PUFFIN BOOKS

The Fiend Next Door

Sheila Lavelle was born in Gateshead, County Durham, in 1939. When she was a child, she spent all her time reading anything she could get her hands on and from the age of ten began to write plays, stories and poetry.

She married in 1958 and had two sons. When her children started school, she returned to the writing that had been put on hold and sold some stories to a magazine. At the same time she trained as a teacher and taught in infant schools for ten years. Sheila Lavelle gave up teaching in 1976 to write full time. Her first book, *Ursula Bear*, was published in 1977.

Sheila Lavelle now lives in a cottage near the sea in Galloway, Scotland, with her husband and two border collies. She is now also a grandmother! Her days are spent writing in the morning and walking her dogs in the afternoon.

THE FIEND
NEXT DOOR

Sheila Lavelle

Illustrated by Margaret Chamberlain

PUFFIN BOOKS

PUFFIN BOOKS

Published by the Penguin Group
Penguin Books Ltd, 27 Wrights Lane, London w8 5tz, England
Penguin Books USA Inc., 375 Hudson Street, New York, New York
10014, USA
Penguin Books Australia Ltd, Ringwood, Victoria, Australia
Penguin Books Canada Ltd, 10 Alcorn Avenue, Toronto, Ontario, Canada m4v 3b2
Penguin Books (NZ) Ltd, 182–190 Wairau Road, Auckland 10, New Zealand

Penguin Books Ltd, Registered Offices: Harmondsworth, Middlesex, England

First published by Hamish Hamilton Ltd 1982
Published in Puffin Books 1995
1 3 5 7 9 10 8 6 4 2

Text copyright © Sheila Lavelle, 1982
Illustrations copyright © Margaret Chamberlain 1995
All rights reserved

The moral right of the author has been asserted

Filmset in Monophoto Baskerville

Printed in England by Clays Ltd, St Ives plc

It was the last day of the holidays and I
didn't want to play with Angela Mitchell
from next door. All I wanted was to spend a
nice peaceful morning, reading a book in my
very own private playshed in the garden. My
dad built the playshed for me when I was
little, and it's got a couple of old chairs and a
table and a furry rug and some shelves and a
great big cupboard where I can keep all my
junk. And it's a lovely place to be on a sunny
September morning because you can open the

window and listen to the birds singing and smell the woodsmoke from my dad's bonfire.

I was just making myself comfortable with a Mars bar and my favourite Roald Dahl story when the shed door suddenly flew open and Angela fell in. And she was in such a state that I couldn't help getting involved, even though I should have known better.

'Charlie!' she burst out. 'I've done something terrible!' She flung herself into the old armchair and put her hands over her face.

My name is Charlotte really, but everybody calls me Charlie. Except Miss Bennett at school. And my mum sometimes when she's especially cross with me because I can't seem to stay out of mischief for five minutes.

Of course I know perfectly well why it is that I keep on getting into so much trouble. My dad is always telling me that it's time I found myself a new best friend and told that Angela Mitchell to get lost. And to be honest I think he's right, because most of the time it's all her fault. Like the time when I was climbing a tree on Cookburn Common and she went off and phoned the fire brigade and they came tearing along in a great big fire engine and I had to pretend I needed rescuing. And the fireman who rescued me was the same one who put out the fire when we burned down Angela's dad's garage last summer. He wasn't pleased to see me again, I can tell you.

I don't think Angela always means to be bad. It just sort of happens. And it seems to happen most often when she's with me. I once wrote in a composition at school, 'Angela Mitchell is my very best FIEND'. It was a stupid spelling mistake, and everybody laughed like mad. But my dad says there's many a true word spoken in jest and if anybody deserves to be called a fiend it's Angela. I don't know why I bother with her, sometimes. And then at other times she can be really nice. You never know where you are. But you're never bored, that's for sure.

Angela is very good at having hysterics. Like the time I cut all her lovely long hair off with her mum's new dressmaking scissors and made her look like a scarecrow. But sometimes it's very hard to tell whether or not Angela's hysterics are real. So I just sat there for a

3

while, staring at her and trying to decide if it was all a fake. Finally I got up and put my arm round her shoulders.

'There, there,' I said. And it seemed a pretty useless sort of thing to say, but it's what everybody says when you get upset even when it doesn't do the slightest bit of good.

'I've done it this time,' she wailed. 'They'll put me in prison and it serves me right. Please, Charlie. You'll have to help me.'

'What've you done now?' I said, and she sobbed and moaned a bit more. I patted her shoulder helplessly.

'Come on, Angela,' I said. 'It can't be all that bad. Whatever it is.' She looked up at me and her eyes were all dark and tragic and filled with tears.

'It is,' she gulped. 'It's the most awfullest, terriblest, dreadfullest thing I've ever done in my whole life!'

Well, that made by blood curdle a bit, I can tell you, because she's done some pretty bad things in her time.

'Worse than putting dead spiders in Miss Menzies' cucumber sandwiches?' I said.

'Much worse than that,' she groaned.

'Worse than setting fire to your dad's garage?' I said fearfully, and Angela gave a great sob.

'TEN times worse than that!' she said. I swallowed hard.

'What then?' I said weakly, not really wanting to hear. Angela took a deep breath.

'I'll get twenty years for sure,' she said hopelessly. 'I've kidnapped a baby. A little baby girl. From outside the supermarket.' And she started to howl all over again.

I stood there with my mouth hanging open and I couldn't think of anything to say. And then I remembered all the times she'd told fibs and played tricks on me and got me to believe all kinds of rubbish.

'I don't believe you,' I said at last. 'I bet you're having me on. Even you wouldn't do a thing like that.'

She didn't answer. Instead she jumped up from her chair, flung open the shed door and pointed outside with a dramatic gesture of her arm. I poked my head out and my heart gave a sort of lurch in my chest.

On the path beside the shed wall was one of those folding baby-buggy pushchairs. And in it was a baby. A pretty little baby girl, in a pink woolly suit and a pink knitted bonnet with a frill around it.

'Oh, no!' I breathed. 'Oh, lord!'

The baby waved her arms and kicked her feet about and made cooing noises when she saw me, and I think she was the nicest baby I have ever seen. She had blue eyes and pink cheeks and little blonde curls peeping out from under her bonnet. Angela must have looked just like that when she was little.

We stood together in the doorway and gazed at the baby without saying anything for a while. Then Angela went out and started dragging the pushchair into the shed.

'You'll have to help me to hide her, Charlie,' she said. 'They'll be searching the whole village.'

And so before I knew what I was doing I had pulled the buggy inside and shut and bolted the door. Angela unfastened the safety harness and lifted the baby out on to the floor. And the baby started to crawl about, pulling things down off the shelves and tipping all the papers out of the rubbish bin. Angela and I sat side by side on an orange crate and watched her, and bit by bit the story came out.

'She was sitting outside the supermarket,' sniffed Angela, blowing her nose. 'And she looked so cute I stopped to say hello. And when she gave me this huge smile I don't know what came over me. I just sort of wanted to keep her for myself. I grabbed the pushchair and ran all the way here. Oh, Charlie,' she cried, clutching my arm. 'Will they send me to Borstal? Will they put me in a horrible grey uniform?'

'They'll put you in a strait-jacket if you ask me,' I said sourly. 'You must be off your head.' I suddenly got to my feet and started to put the baby back in the buggy.

'Come on, Angela,' I said firmly. 'This has gone on long enough. You've got to take her back. And the sooner the better. If you're lucky they may not have called the police yet.'

But when I mentioned the police Angela got all in a panic and started sobbing and moaning all over again.

'You do it,' she begged. 'Please, Charlie! You take her back. I just daren't.'

'NOT BLOOMING LIKELY!' I shouted. And I wasn't half mad, I can tell you. 'I'm not getting the blame! I'm not that stupid, Angela Mitchell!' We both sat down and glared at each other.

By now the baby was getting bored with playing by herself and was starting to whimper a bit. I picked her up to give her a cuddle, but she wriggled fretfully in my arms and sucked noisily at her fist.

'She's hungry,' I said crossly to Angela. 'Now what are we going to do?'

'Get some milk and biscuits from your mum,' she said, as cool as anything. 'It's about time for elevenses, anyway.'

I scowled at her. 'Why me?' I said. 'Why can't you ask your mum? It's all your fault in the first place.'

'I can't,' said Angela. 'My mum's got a visitor. And you know how she hates me to pester her when she's having one of her coffee mornings. Go on, Charlie. Your mum won't mind.'

I grumbled a bit more, but I had to go in the end. Not to please Angela, but because the baby was really crying hard and I thought somebody might hear her.

'Get your mum to warm the milk, Charlie,' Angela shouted after me as I hurried up the garden towards the house.

My mum was in the kitchen mixing a cake. The electric mixer was on and Leo Sayer was singing at full volume on the record player and I had trouble making her understand what I wanted.

'What?' she said. 'Milk and biscuits? For you and Angela? Yes, all right. But you'll have to help yourself, sweetheart. I'm a bit busy at the moment.'

So I put a few biscuits on a tray and poured some milk into a small saucepan on the stove. My mum switched off the noisy mixer and raised her eyebrows at me.

'You don't like hot milk, Charlie,' she reminded me. 'What are you doing that for?'

'I'm just er . . . warming it a bit,' I said, feeling my face go pink. 'It's a bit chilly this morning.'

My mum looked out of the window at the

blue sky and the sunshine and shook her head in a baffled way.

'Please yourself,' she shrugged. 'But don't leave dirty saucepans for me to clear up, will you. I've got enough to do as it is.'

So after I had poured the warm milk into two plastic beakers I had to wash the saucepan and dry it and put it away. I put the milk on the tray and opened the back door and just at that moment the record came to an end and everything went quiet and you could hear the baby crying in the distance.

'What's that?' said my mum, holding the door for me so that I could use both hands for the tray. 'Surely you haven't got a baby down in the shed?'

I gave a funny sort of giggle.

'A what?' I said. 'A baby? Good heavens, no. It's only Angela. We're playing, er . . . a sort of game.' And I fled down the path with the cups wobbling like mad and a nasty shaky feeling in my stomach because I hate telling fibs to anybody. Especially my mum.

Angela pulled me into the shed and slammed the door.

'You've been ages,' she complained. 'The baby's frantic. What took you so long?'

I didn't bother to explain. I sat the baby on my lap and held a beaker of milk to her mouth. She stopped howling at once and began to gulp it down, clutching at the beaker with both hands. We hardly spilt any at all, and before long the beaker was empty. Angela sat and watched us, grinning and munching my mum's homemade shortbread biscuits.

'We're taking this baby back,' I said. 'I'll just have to come with you, I suppose, since you won't go yourself. Have you thought about what sort of state the baby's mother must be in by now? I don't know how you can sit there grinning like that.'

Angela jumped up at once.

'You'll really go with me?' she said, all smiles. 'Charlie, you're the best friend I ever had.'

I strapped the baby back in her buggy and gave her a biscuit to chew.

'We'll put her back outside the supermarket,' I said. 'Maybe nobody'll see us. But mind,

I'm not taking any of the blame if we're caught.'

The baby seemed a lot happier now, cooing and gurgling and kicking her feet about, and she didn't seem to mind a bit when I put a big straw hat on her head and covered her from neck to feet in an old stripey blanket that almost reached the ground.

'What's that for?' said Angela. 'Oh, I see. It's a disguise. Charlie Ellis, you are clever!'

'You and me next,' I told her. 'We don't want to be recognized either.'

So we rummaged about in my dressing-up box and found some old clothes to cover our own. I wore a pair of dark sunglasses and a cowboy hat and a long velvet cloak down to my feet. And Angela wore my Auntie Vida's old fur coat and the black wig my dad made when he went to the tennis club Hallowe'en party as a witch. In the end we all looked so funny I just had to giggle, even though I was scared to death and sure we were going to get arrested any minute.

Angela kindly offered to let me push the buggy, would you believe, but I wasn't having any of that. So off we went down the path and into the street, with Angela pushing the buggy and me looking nervously around for panda cars.

Well, we didn't get very far, I can tell you. In fact we only got as far as Angela's front gate. And suddenly there was Angela's mum coming out of the house with her visitor.

And in spite of being so worried I couldn't help staring, because even though I'd never seen that lady in my life before I could tell straight away who she was. I've never seen two people more alike. They were as alike as a pair of socks. It could only be Auntie Sally's sister from Canada.

Anyway, they both looked astonished when they saw us in our weird clothes. They raised their eyebrows at one another and then they burst out laughing.

'Whatever are you up to?' said Angela's mum. 'We were just on our way to find you. What are you all dressed up like this for?'

My knees were shaking a bit and I thought I'd leave it to Angela to make up some sort of story. But I couldn't believe my eyes when I looked at her, because she was grinning all over her face and didn't look bothered in the least.

The other lady knelt down and took the rug off the baby's shoulders.

'Hello, my little poppet,' she said, in that soppy cooing voice that grown-ups always use when they speak to babies, as if babies were all halfwitted. 'Did Sarah Jane have a lovely time with her cousin Angela, then? Did you miss your mummy, darling?' Then she turned to Angela with a smile.

'Thanks for looking after her, Angela,' she said. 'Your mum and I had time for a nice long chat, and it was lovely to catch up on all the news. I expect we'll see quite a lot of you now we've moved to Barlow. Has Sarah Jane been any trouble?'

Angela shook her head.

'She's been as good as gold,' she said, her eyes all sparkly with mischief. 'We've been playing a fantastic game, pretending we were kidnappers wanted by the police and hiding in Charlie's old shed and getting dressed up in disguises and stuff. Haven't we, Charlie?'

I nodded dumbly. There didn't seem a lot I could say. I felt a proper fool, and I went on standing there with my mouth hanging open like an idiot while Angela's mum introduced her twin sister Beth, who had been living in Canada for ten years and that was why I had never seen the baby before.

And then off they all went, laughing and chattering together, to have lunch at the Wimpy bar, leaving me in the street all by myself with my arms full of disguises. I trudged off home swearing to myself that I'd get my own back one of these days, and I gave Angela's gatepost a good kick on the way past which didn't do any good at all.

I was in a rotten temper when I got home, but suddenly I felt much better, because I found that my dad had come home unexpectedly for lunch and had brought fish and chips in with him from that nice new fish and chip shop down the road.

So while we were eating fish and chips and tomato ketchup and bread and butter I started to tell my mum and dad all about what had happened. And somehow the more I told it the funnier it sounded until we were all falling about laughing and wiping our eyes and shaking our heads and saying what a villain Angela was and all of a sudden I wasn't a bit mad with her any longer.

2

Angela isn't always horrible to me, though. Sometimes she's very kind and generous. She lets me ride her lovely new yellow bike whenever I want to, and I can read her comics every Saturday after she's read them first. I'm not allowed to buy comics because my mum doesn't approve of them and I don't think it's a bit fair. They're no worse than some of the soppy magazines she reads with all that awful love stuff and Mary Moan's Problem Page. My dad tells her it wouldn't do her any harm to read a good book for a change, but my mum says what about him and his football paper and that shuts him up.

Every morning in term-time Angela calls for me and we walk to school together, even though we're not allowed to sit together in class. Miss Bennett always used to say we brought out the worst in each other. And even in Miss Bridge's class we've been put at opposite sides of the room. I have to sit next to that awful spiteful cat Delilah Jones, and Angela doesn't seem to mind a bit. She sits next to David Watkins, and he's the nicest boy in the class. I wouldn't even mind marrying David Watkins when I grow up.

I shouldn't have told Angela that, though. She went and spread it round the whole school. She even chalked it on the wall of the boys' loos, 'Charlie Ellis loves David Watkins'. And now he goes as red as a pillar box whenever I speak to him.

Angela is going to marry Keanu Reeves when she grows up because he's a rich film star. She used to like Prince William, but she suddenly went off him for no reason. I was glad when that happened, because Angela gave me all her scrapbooks with his photos in. My dad told her she was fickle, but she only laughed.

Anyway, we hadn't been in our new class five minutes before Angela started getting me into trouble. And it was a bright idea of Miss Bridge's that caused the whole thing. She's one of those keen and with-it teachers straight out of college and crazy about Projects and Activities and Learning by Experience and stuff like that. She doesn't just write things on the blackboard and make you copy them while she dozes at her desk like all the other teachers do. It makes you wonder what some of them get paid for sometimes.

The lesson was Nature Study, and we were all a bit bored and sleepy because it was Friday and a warm September afternoon. I was wishing the lesson was over so Angela and I could go blackberry picking on the common. I'd promised my mum I'd try to get enough to mix with some of our apples for a pie. She makes lovely blackberry and apple pies, my mum does, with the sort of pastry that melts in your mouth and loads of thick cream. No wonder my dad's getting so fat.

Miss Bridge was talking about pets, and she was asking the children in the class about the different sorts of animals they kept at home and what they fed them on and that sort of thing.

'Please, Miss Bridge, we've got a dog called Hector,' said that fat Laurence Parker, putting up his hand. 'We used to have a goldfish as well, but we had to get rid of it because of the noise.'

We all stared at him and somebody started to snigger. Miss Bridge's eyebrows nearly disappeared into her fringe.

'The goldfish made too much noise?' she said. 'Surely not.'

'No, Miss,' said Laurence. 'The dog did. It kept on barking at the goldfish.'

We all giggled like anything and even Miss Bridge had to smile. Then when we'd calmed down a bit she turned to me.

'What about you, Charlie?' she said. 'Have you got a pet?' And of course I'd been dreading that question because my pet isn't anything to boast about, but it's the only kind my mum will let me have as she can't bear animals' hairs all over the place.

'Well . . . um . . . er . . . I've got a tortoise,' I said at last.

'How nice,' said Miss Bridge politely, in that special grown-up sort of voice that really means 'how boring'. 'Is it a girl or a boy?'

Well honestly, what a stupid question. How is anybody supposed to tell whether a tortoise is a boy or a girl? I certainly can't tell the difference and my mum and dad can't tell the difference, and I bet you anything that Miss Bridge couldn't tell the difference, either. Even the vet has trouble.

'We think it's a boy,' I said, hoping she'd leave it at that. But this wasn't my lucky day.

'And what is his name?' went on Miss Bridge relentlessly. The question I'd been dreading most of all.

There was a muffled splutter of laughter from somewhere behind me and I knew it was Angela because she's the only one who knows. Everybody was waiting and I went all pink and hung my head and shuffled my feet and said nothing.

'What's the matter, Charlie?' said Miss Bridge, getting a bit impatient. 'You haven't forgotten your own pet's name?'

I was just making up my mind to tell a fib and say Fred or George or something like that when there was the sound of a chair scraping on the floor and Angela stood up.

'Please, Miss Bridge,' she said, and she could hardly speak for giggling. 'I know what Charlie's tortoise is called. Charlie's tortoise is called ROVER!'

I could have killed her. Everybody hooted with laughter and in the end Miss Bridge had to bang on her desk lid with the blackboard ruler. And then I had to explain all about my mum not letting me have a dog because of hairs on the carpets, so a tortoise called Rover seemed the next best thing.

And to my surprise Miss Bridge was quite sympathetic.

'I quite understand, Charlie,' she said gently, even though her mouth was twitching and I could tell she was dying to laugh, too.

'Perhaps you'll be able to have a dog later on. When you are old enough to look after it yourself.'

'Yes, Miss Bridge,' I said. 'I hope so.' I sat down thankfully and did my best to ignore the rude faces that awful Delilah Jones was making at me.

'Well now,' said Miss Bridge, smiling round at the class. 'This little chat has given me a good idea. The next few Fridays can be Pet Afternoons. I'll choose one person each week to bring their pet to school. And they can prepare a little talk about it for the rest of the class.'

You should have heard the moans and groans, and one or two people called out that they had no pets at all. Miss Bridge held up her hand.

'The animal doesn't have to be your own,' she said. 'I won't mind if you borrow one from a relative or a friend. Try to get hold of some interesting, unusual sort of pet. But of course you must be sensible. We don't want donkeys or Saint Bernard dogs in the classroom.'

'Oh, Miss,' said Laurence Parker, sounding all disappointed. 'Can't I bring my killer whale?' And this time even Miss Bridge joined in the laughter. Laurence Parker does say some funny things sometimes.

'I'd really rather you didn't, Laurence,' said Miss Bridge, when the noise died down. 'But you can be first with your pet next Friday. We shall all be looking forward to a nice, interesting talk.'

The bell went for the end of afternoon school and Miss Bridge dismissed us. We all went trooping out, and Angela and I collected our belongings from the cloakroom.

'I hope Miss Bridge doesn't pick me for one of her Pet Afternoons,' I said gloomily, as we set off towards the common. 'I'd die if I had to bring Rover to school. I'd feel a proper fool.' Angela pushed her arm through mine.

'Well, I hope she chooses me,' she said. 'I wouldn't mind a bit.'

I stared at her in surprise.

'Why not?' I said. 'All you've got is a jam-jar with a dead caterpillar in it. I don't call that very interesting or unusual.'

She let go of my arm and began to hopscotch along the pavement.

'You know my Uncle Quentin who went to Oxford to study zoology?' she said over her shoulder. 'Well, he's got a job now at the London Zoo. And they often lend animals for things like school projects. I bet he could get me a nice little baby monkey or something.'

'He couldn't,' I said. 'You're making it up. How could he bring it all the way from London Zoo?'

'I bet he could,' she said. 'He only lives at Barlow. He could call with it on his way home. I'm going to ask him, anyway. So there.' And she went skipping off, leaving me to trudge dolefully along behind.

The next Friday came round and Laurence Parker turned up with a box of silkworms. You might not think silkworms are all that exciting, but he made his talk so interesting that everybody got fascinated with the funny little creatures and we were having such a great time that the afternoon was over before we knew it.

After that we had terrapins, a baby rabbit,

a cageful of stick insects, a talking mynah bird that kept saying a rude word over and over again until Miss Bridge had to put a cloth over its cage, and somebody even brought a tame hedgehog that snored loudly in its box all through the lesson. It didn't look as though Miss Bridge was going to pick me, after all, and I started to look forward to Friday afternoons.

Then it was Angela's turn, and she went home for lunch that day so she could pick up the animal her Uncle Quentin had brought. She wouldn't tell anybody what it was, not even me, and when she turned up in the afternoon with a small brown basket I could tell by her face that it was something very special.

And it was. Angela opened the lid of the basket and lifted out a sleepy, furry bundle with a long, black and white striped tail and a little pointed face with big ears.

'It's a ring-tailed lemur,' she said smugly. 'His name's Ringo.' And everybody fell in love with it at once.

You should have heard all the oohs and

aahs. The lemur sat on Angela's shoulder while she gave her talk, and I think her Uncle Quentin must have given her some help with that as well because she could never have made it up herself. It was all about marsupials and the rain forests of Madagascar and it was just as good as David Attenborough on the telly.

Miss Bridge was as pleased as anything and she let everybody stroke the lemur before it went back into its basket. It was the friendliest creature you ever saw, because it had once been somebody's pet before it went to live in the zoo, and I couldn't help wishing I could keep it for myself.

'Thank you, Angela,' said Miss Bridge, beaming all over her face. 'A charming animal, and a most interesting talk. I'm delighted that you all seem to be responding so well to this project. Now, we just have time for one more pet before we break up for half-term.'

Her eyes swept around the class and my heart sank because I suddenly knew who she was going to choose.

'Charlie Ellis,' said Miss Bridge with a smile. 'We haven't had your little pet, have we?'

I did my best to argue myself out of it, but she wouldn't listen.

'Tortoises are extremely interesting creatures,' she said. 'And I know you can make your talk well worth listening to. I don't want to hear any more excuses.'

And so that was that. I felt really fed up, I can tell you. Even though Angela let me carry the basket with the lemur in it on the way home.

'How can I possibly take Rover to school?' I said in despair. 'Can you imagine it? They'll all laugh their silly heads off. Especially that fat Laurence Parker and that spiteful Delilah Jones.'

Angela put her arm round my shoulders.

'Cheer up, Charlie,' she said. 'I could always get my Uncle Quentin to borrow something for you, too.'

I stopped dead in the middle of the pavement and stared at her. I could hardly believe my ears.

'Do you think he would?' I said breathlessly.

'I don't see why not,' she replied, pushing

her hair back from her face. 'He's coming over tonight to collect Ringo. I'll ask him then if you like.'

Well, when Angela came round later that evening to tell me that the answer was yes, I was so pleased and excited and relieved and grateful that I could have hugged her.

'That's all right, Charlie,' she said carelessly. 'You know what they say about a friend in need. But you can do my maths homework for me in exchange, if you like.'

I told my dad about it when we were having supper that night, and my dad said I should watch it. Angela Mitchell could be up to something, we all know what she's like, he told me. But my mum said it was wrong of him always to think the worst of Angela, and maybe she really meant to be a good friend this time. That made my dad choke on his sausages and mash, and I had to bang him on the back for five whole minutes.

And of course I should have listened to him because he's usually right, especially about things like that, but I went blithely off to bed and dreamed about all the lovely things that

Angela's Uncle Quentin might bring me from the zoo. It could be a bush-baby, I thought, or a nice little owl, or even a koala bear.

But the week went by and Thursday came and still I hadn't found out what sort of animal I was getting. Angela's uncle was away at a conference for a few days, she said, and wouldn't be back until Friday morning.

'He's bringing the animal to my house at lunch time,' she explained. 'I'll go home for lunch and pick it up for you.'

'That's no good,' I said crossly. 'How am I supposed to prepare a talk when I don't even know what it's about?'

'I'm sorry, Charlie,' she said, and she really sounded as if she meant it. 'It's the best I can do. Do you want to forget the whole thing and just bring Rover instead?'

I shook my head hurriedly.

'Not likely,' I said. 'Anything but that. I'll just have to manage somehow.'

And on Friday afternoon of course Angela was late for school. The bell had gone and we were all in our places and I was worried half out of my wits when she came rushing breathlessly in and pushed a smallish wooden box into my hands.

'What is it?' I hissed frantically, but the teacher was coming into the room so Angela had to slip away to her place and sit down.

'Good afternoon, everybody,' said Miss Bridge, and we all clattered to our feet.

'Good afternoon, Miss Bridge,' we chorused politely. Then we all sat down again and the lesson began.

I stared at the box on the desk in front of me. It was about the size of a shoe box and it had a sliding lid with air holes drilled through. I was relieved that it looked so small. At least Angela hadn't brought me a crocodile.

I inched back the lid just a fraction and tried to peer inside, but it was all dark in there and I couldn't make out a thing. Then Miss Bridge's voice made me jump.

'Charlie! You're keeping us all waiting,' she said. So I got up and carried the box to the front of the class.

Everybody went very quiet and gazed at me expectantly. I looked at Angela hoping she would give me some sort of a clue, but she kept her head down and I couldn't see her face. I cleared my throat nervously. The room was so silent you could have heard a feather fall.

'Er ... um ... well,' I stuttered. 'This animal is a ...' I slid open the lid of the box and the whole class craned forward to look.

I think it was one of the horriblest moments of my life. I went stiff and cold all over and the hairs on the back of my neck went prickly and I shuddered with fright as I stared down at the THING in the box.

It had an ugly black furry body and an ugly black leathery face and great nasty black wings with claws on the ends. It was the ugliest creature I had ever seen.

'Ugh! It's a BAT!' I said, and my voice came out all croaky.

Angela knows there are two things I can't stand at any price. One of them is spiders, and the other is bats. They make me go all funny just to look at them, and it's no good anybody telling me that they're perfectly harmless little creatures. I can't help it if they make me think of graveyards and vampires and Dracula and blood and witches and dark cobwebby towers and creepy things like that. I imagine their claws tangled in my hair and their sharp little teeth biting my neck and I go goose-pimply all over and my dad says I read too many spooky books.

Anyway, this bat must have been disturbed by the light because it suddenly stretched out its great black wings and hopped out of the box on to my wrist. I felt its cold claws gripping my skin and that was the last straw. I dropped the box with a clatter and started to scream my head off.

'Blimey! It's a bloomin' vampire!' shouted that fat fool Laurence Parker, and that started everybody else off screaming, too. And it was sheer bedlam in the classroom with everybody leaping out of their desks and charging about bumping into one another and fighting to get to the door and diving under tables and things. And the bat made things ten times worse by swooping about and banging itself into the walls and windows and Miss Bridge didn't help much by yelling and thumping on her desk but there was so much noise that nobody took any notice of her anyway.

And of course in the end it was Angela who did the sensible thing. She climbed up on to the window ledge with the box in her hands and sort of scooped the bat into it from the corner of the glass. Then she shut the lid and put it safely back on the teacher's desk.

Miss Bridge was standing there with her arms folded grimly and her face all red and I could tell she was furious. Everybody started shuffling back to their places with sheepish little grins and of course most of them hadn't been frightened at all but just thought it was a good excuse for a bit of a riot.

We all had to stay silent for the rest of the lesson and Miss Bridge made us write a composition about Self Control. I was more relieved than sorry because I couldn't have given a talk on bats to save my life. But of course I got kept in after school and given a good old telling-off about silly behaviour and causing a disturbance and stuff like that.

'It would have been better to have brought your tortoise,' said Miss Bridge crossly, 'than to risk that sort of panic in the classroom. Do try to think more sensibly in future, Charlie.'

Angela was waiting for me when I came out of the gate but I refused to speak to her. Even when she tried to explain that the bat was a harmless fruit-bat from South America and was as tame as a kitten. I shoved the box into her hands and said I never wanted to see it, or her, ever again. And this time I managed to keep my word for a whole weekend.

3

It wasn't my idea to hijack the milkman's float. I didn't like the sound of it in the least, and I told Angela so.

'Hijacking's against the law,' I said. 'People get put in prison for hijacking things. You can read about it in the papers every day.'

We were sunbathing on a rug in Angela's front garden. Mr Wood, the milkman, had just gone inside for a cup of coffee with Angela's dad. He had left his milk float parked in the street by the gate.

'Knickers!' said Angela, pushing her fringe out of her eyes. 'That's only if it's a plane or an ocean liner or something big like that. What about the bloke who hijacked the number twenty-three bus in Barlow the other day? He made the driver take him all the way to Budgen's for a packet of teabags. And the judge only gave him a suspenders sentence, whatever that is.'

'I don't like it,' I said. 'We'll get into trouble.'

'Soppy old spoilsport!' said Angela. 'Tell you what, then. We won't hijack it. We'll just move it a few yards down the street. Then when Mr Wood comes out he'll think it's been stolen. It'll be the funniest thing you ever saw!'

She began to giggle and hop up and down on the lawn, and before I knew what was happening I was giggling, too. And once I started doing that I knew it was no use trying to argue with her. Not that arguing with Angela ever does any good anyway.

'Come on, Charlie,' she said, pulling me to my feet. 'Be a sport.' And I didn't have the heart to say no.

There was still no sign of the milkman coming out so we walked down the drive into the street. The milk float stood neatly against the kerb and its yellow and white paint was all shiny in the sun. There wasn't a lot of milk left because it was eleven o'clock in the morning and the round was nearly finished, but there were hundreds of crates of empty bottles. Angela stuck her head in the cab.

'That's the accelerator,' she said, pointing to a button on the floor. 'And that's the brake pedal. And this cable thing is the hand brake. Come on, Charlie. Hop in.'

I was a bit scared, but I didn't say so to Angela. She's always going on at me for being a scaredy-cat so I have to pretend I'm as brave as she is.

I walked slowly round the float and climbed into the cab on the passenger side. Angela scrambled into the driver's seat and grinned at me. I tried to smile back but my face felt all stiff and funny.

'You don't know how to drive it,' I said, hopefully.

''Course I do, stupid,' she said. 'It's easy as

pie. I've watched Mr Wood loads of times when I was little and he used to give me rides down the street. Anyway, there's no need to drive it at all. We only have to take the hand brake off and it'll start rolling down the hill by itself. We can stop it a few yards away and walk back. You can hardly call that hijacking, now can you?'

When she put it like that it didn't sound too bad. I looked towards the house but there was nobody in sight. It was Saturday, both our mums were at the hairdresser's, my dad was busy mowing our back lawn, and the whole street looked quiet. I suddenly wished I was round the back helping my dad in the garden, instead of sitting here with Angela getting into another load of trouble.

'Right then. Here we go,' said Angela, and she pressed a little knob on the hand brake and pushed the lever down.

My stomach seemed to sink inside me as I felt the milk float start to roll silently forward. Our part of the street is on quite a gentle slope but it gets a lot steeper near the bottom, and there's a sharp bend at the end before it meets the main road. So I was a bit worried in case we let it roll too far and ended up on the steep bit. I put my hands over my face and shut my eyes.

'I think that's far enough, Angela,' I pleaded. 'We'd better stop now.'

The cart went on rolling and I could sense that it was gaining speed.

'Please, Angela,' I said. 'Let's stop.' Then I heard a sort of scuffle and a thump, so I opened my eyes to see what she was up to.

Well, I got such a fright I nearly had kittens. Angela wasn't there. I was sitting in that cab all by myself and it was racing away down the hill getting faster and faster and all I could think about was that great big brick wall at the bottom where the road went round the corner.

'Angela!' I shouted. I swivelled round in my seat and just managed to catch a glimpse of her through the pile of crates in the back. There she was, picking herself up off the pavement and brushing the dust off her pink denim dungarees.

'Hang on, Charlie!' she shouted back. 'I'll

get help.' And she started to run up the street towards the house.

I gritted my teeth and said a very rude word because I knew very well that she wasn't really going for help at all. She was dashing off to find the milkman and tell him that terrible Charlie Ellis was hijacking his float. But I didn't have time to worry about that now. There was a brick wall rushing towards me at a hundred miles an hour and I knew I'd better do something quick or there'd be an almighty crash. And then even Angela would be sorry.

I grabbed the handle on the hand brake and gave it a heave. Nothing happened. I couldn't budge it at all. It was too stiff, or else the cart was just going too fast. I scrambled across into the driver's seat and looked down at the two pedals on the floor. One was the accelerator and one was the brake. But which was which?

I put my foot fearfully on the pedal on the right and pressed gently. And that's when I almost died of fright because that started the electric motor and made me go even faster.

The cart swayed and jolted and the motor whined and all the crates were rattling about like mad behind me and I could see the astonished faces of people in the street as I went whizzing by.

The brick wall was only yards away by now. And I don't know how I did it but I got my foot on that brake pedal just in time. I stamped on the pedal as hard as I could and I wrenched the steering wheel hard over to the left and the tyres squealed as the milk float went hurtling round the bend missing the wall by inches and finally lurching to a sudden stop that sent all the crates crashing into one another and almost flung me through the windscreen. But I had stopped the cart. And I was still breathing. And I felt as proud of myself as if I'd won an Olympic gold medal.

I felt very shaky though, and at first I couldn't get out of the cab. I was just sort of sitting there, getting my breath back and mopping my hot face with my hanky, when I heard a lot of commotion and loud voices behind me. I looked round, and there was

Angela. With the milkman. And her dad. And my dad. And they all looked furious.

My dad reached into the cab and yanked me out and held me so tight I couldn't even breathe. And I think he was so relieved to find that I was all right that he couldn't speak a word. Everybody else made up for it, though, and do you know, not one of them asked me what had happened. They just went on yelling and arguing amongst themselves, and a crowd of neighbours started gathering in the street to see what was going on. You could tell by their faces that half of them were disappointed there wasn't any blood.

And in the end it was Angela who actually spoke to me first.

'Ooh, Charlie Ellis!' she said, her blue eyes all wide and her voice all shocked. 'You are naughty! What a thing to do!'

I was so mad I was speechless. And even when I got my voice back I couldn't tell on her, because you shouldn't tell tales, especially on your best friend. She got off scot free, and once again I took all the blame. But I swore in my heart that I would get even with that Angela Mitchell one day, if it was the last thing I did.

4

I called round at Angela's house one blowy
afternoon in May to see if she wanted to fly
my new kite with me on the common. My dad
had made the kite for me out of bamboo canes
and brown paper and I had been waiting for a
nice windy day to try it out. I really wanted
my dad to go with me, but of course I should
have known better than to ask. It was Saturday, and there was football on the telly.

'Hello, Charlie,' said Auntie Sally, when I
knocked on their back door. 'I'm just blow-

drying Angela's hair. Why don't you go and have a chat with Uncle Jim until she's ready? I think he's out in the greenhouse.'

I thought that was a good idea. If Angela was having her hair done I would probably have to wait for ever. She's got the kind of long, thick hair that takes hours and hours to dry, and she's ever so fussy about getting her curls in the right place. You'd think she was a film star or something.

I found Angela's dad in the greenhouse watering some of his plants. And it was lovely in his greenhouse because he's a very clever gardener and the place was full of carnations and freesias and geraniums and stuff like that. He gave me a big grin as I stood there sniffing all the nice scents.

'Do you like gardening, Charlie?' he said.

'Well, I help my dad a bit sometimes,' I replied.

Uncle Jim gave a sort of snort.

'I don't call that gardening,' he said scornfully. 'He only grows a few onions and cabbages. Anybody can do that.'

I didn't think that was very kind. My dad

doesn't know much about flowers, but he does grow some very good vegetables and fruit. He once grew a marrow so big I could sit on its back as if it was a pony.

'He's too interested in his stomach, your dad is,' said Uncle Jim. 'Only grows what he can eat. What you might call marrow-minded.' He gave a great guffaw at his own joke, the way all grown-ups do. 'Look at these geraniums, now,' he went on. 'It's growing things like that gives you a real thrill.'

I looked at them and I could see what he meant. The flowers were huge, and they were all shades of pink and orange and red.

'They're very pretty,' I said. 'Are they hard to grow?'

'Not a bit,' said Uncle Jim. 'Tell you what, Charlie. Why don't you have a go? I'll show you how to take a cutting, if you like.'

I only said yes to be polite, really. But in no time I found I was enjoying myself, and I could tell that Uncle Jim was as happy as anything to have somebody showing some interest in his flowers for a change. He showed me where to snip off a young, leafy shoot, and we

47

mixed up some sandy soil to put in the pot. I made a little hole in the soil with a pencil, popped the cutting in and firmed the soil with my fingers.

'There,' said Uncle Jim. 'It's as easy as that. Give it a drop of water and keep it on a sunny window sill, and in a few months' time it'll be as big as these.'

The greenhouse door slid open just then and Angela stuck her head in. She was wearing her white dress with the yellow spots on and she had a yellow hairband on her clean, shiny hair. She was eating an apple.

'Who do you think you are?' she said, turning her nose up at my grubby hands. 'Alan blooming Titchmarsh?'

'Charlie's going in for horticulture in a big way,' said Uncle Jim. 'Aren't you, Charlie?'

I showed Angela my cutting and told her what we had been doing.

'Why don't you have a go, too?' I said.

'Pooh! Not likely!' said Angela. 'Catch me getting all filthy like that. Who wants to grow a soppy little thing like a geranium, anyway. I'm going to grow an apple tree.'

Angela's dad started to explain that an apple tree would take years to grow, but she took no notice. She fished one of the pips out of her apple and poked it into a spare pot of soil.

'You'll never get apples from that,' said Uncle Jim. But Angela only tossed her head.

'Come on, Charlie,' she said, tugging my arm. 'We've got better things to do.' So I left my cutting to be collected later and we set off towards the common with my kite.

'Don't get your clean clothes messed up,' called Angela's mum as we left. 'And don't be late for tea, please, Angela. Miss Menzies is coming.'

'Not again!' groaned Angela. 'That's made my day!'

She cheered up though when we got to the common, because it was great weather for kite-flying and my new kite went like a bird. We had the time of our lives making it swoop and soar and glide right up above the treetops, and the sun was shining and the wind was blowing in our faces and we both had pink cheeks from all the fresh air and running about.

'Your dad's the best kite-maker that ever was!' puffed Angela, beaming all over her face. And I felt as proud and pleased as could be, because Angela has never said anything as nice as that about my dad. She usually only says horrible things, like the time in the café in Birmingham when she told somebody he'd just come out of a lunatic asylum.

Anyway, we were having such a lot of fun and we didn't squabble once, and the time went by so quickly that it seemed as if the afternoon was over before it had started.

'It must be getting on for tea time,' said Angela. 'I know it's a shame, but I daren't be late after what my mum said. Especially when the slender Miss Menzies is coming to tea.' And we both giggled and made faces at each other, because Miss Menzies is fat and greedy and my dad says you could feed a family of refugees for a week on what she eats at one meal.

By now the kite was very high in the sky so I started to wind in the string. And that's when something happened that spoilt our whole lovely day. A great gust of wind suddenly caught the kite and sent it crashing into the top of one of the tallest elms.

'Now look what's happened,' I said crossly. 'It's got itself stuck.'

The kite was stuck good and proper. The harder we tugged on the string the tighter it jammed itself into the branches, and in the end we tugged so hard that the string snapped.

'Oh, come on,' said Angela impatiently. 'Leave it, Charlie. It's only a tatty old home-made thing anyway. Your dad can make another one, for Pete's sake.'

I don't know who Pete was and why every-body does everything for his sake. And I didn't want my dad to make another kite, not for anybody's sake.

'I want that one,' I said stubbornly. 'It's the best kite I ever had. You can do what you like, Angela Mitchell, but I'm going to get it down.' And without waiting to argue I pulled myself up on to the lowest branch and started to climb.

Angela stood at the bottom and watched me with her mouth open. She's scared stiff of heights and couldn't climb a tree to save her life. She gets dizzy standing on a matchbox. But I love climbing, especially whizzing up and down the ropes in the gym, and Laurence Parker says it's not hard to tell who my ancestors were.

Anyway, this tree was the easiest I had ever climbed, with lots of strong branches to hang on to, and lots of forks to sit astride and get your breath back. I climbed steadily on, not looking down if I could help it, and it wasn't long before I reached the branch where the kite was jammed. It only took a minute to untangle the string and shake it free, and I was dead pleased with myself, I can tell you, when I sent the kite floating to the ground. I looked down to wave to Angela, but she was nowhere to be seen.

'That's just like her,' I grumbled to myself. 'She's gone off and left me. Why couldn't she have waited?' I didn't really mind all that much, though, because I knew she was worried about being late for tea. So I thought while I was up there I might as well have a look at the view.

I hauled myself on to the highest branch and the view was fantastic. I could see every bit of the common and the River Thames with a few sailing boats on it and all the roofs of the houses at Edgebourne and some black and white cows in a field at Lunnon's Farm and the church spire sticking up in the distance. And at the edge of the common where it joins the main road I could see the red telephone box with a white and yellow blob coming out of it.

I blinked and stared and shielded my eyes from the sun to see better, because that white and yellow blob looked very much like Angela from here. And when it started running across the common towards my tree I realised that it *was* Angela. What could she have been doing in the telephone box?

I very soon found out. I heard the noise of the siren first, and then I saw it. A great big red fire engine, hurtling along the road from Edgebourne, with coiled-up water hoses and huge long ladders and about a million firemen all in their smart uniforms and helmets.

Angela shouted and waved at the firemen

and pointed her arm in the direction of my tree. The fire engine left the road and came bouncing and rattling over the rough grass and bushes towards me and all I could do was cling to my branch and say rude words about Angela under my breath. I couldn't start climbing down because then they'd have known it was a hoax and we'd both have been in trouble.

So I stayed meekly where I was while the fire engine stopped under my tree and all the firemen got out and stood around waving their arms about and arguing. Then one of those great long extending ladders came sliding up towards my branch with a fat ginger-haired fireman hanging on the end of it. And I very nearly did fall out of the tree when I saw him, because it was the same man who had put out the fire when Angela and I burnt down Uncle Jim's garage last summer, and I could tell by his face that he recognised me, too.

'You again, is it?' was all he said, and I nodded dumbly. I didn't speak a word. I just let myself be dragged out of the tree and carried over his shoulder like a sack of potatoes while he backed down the ladder and I didn't half feel stupid. And when I was safely on the ground I went straight to Angela and trod on her foot as hard as I could.

Angela pretended not to notice. She was too busy flinging her arms around me and prancing about like a maniac because my life had been saved and honestly, I could have killed her. But of course I had to thank everybody politely and say how sorry I was to be a nuisance.

We had an awful job getting rid of them, though. They wanted to take us home after my terrible ordeal, and I had to insist that I was all right. I didn't fancy the idea of arriving in the street in a fire engine, and I could see that Angela didn't, either. Then they had to take our names and addresses for their report, and that took ages, and more and more nosy people were arriving to find out what was going on and I was getting more and more fidgety and fed-up.

But at last they did go. And I was so relieved to get away at last that we ran all the way home. It was only when we reached my gate that I realised what we'd done.

'The kite!' I said breathlessly. 'I've left the kite behind.'

Angela giggled. 'After all that!' she said. 'Charlie, you're hopeless.' Then she gave me a grin. 'Never mind,' she said. 'I'll go back with you after tea to get it.' And off she went.

She kept her word, too. She came round about half-past six. She brought my geranium cutting that I'd left in the greenhouse, and in her other hand was a pot with a nice little tree in it. A small apple tree, all covered in pink and white blossom.

'What's that?' I said.

'Oh, just my apple tree,' she said casually. 'Remember the pip I planted this morning? It's doing quite well, isn't it?'

Then she collapsed into giggles. 'Oh, Charlie!' she said. 'I wish you could see your face!'

And of course it was only an apple tree branch that she'd broken off and stuck in the pot to fool me. But it looked so real it soon had me giggling as well.

'Come on, Charlie,' she said. 'Let's go and show it to my dad.'

And off we went together, arm in arm. It's funny how I can't stay mad with her for more than five minutes.

5

Every Monday afternoon in Miss Bridge's class we have a lesson called Story Time. Each of us in turn has to read aloud to the rest of the class, and you mustn't read out of a book because the story has to be one that you've written yourself. Sometimes it's so boring you could almost fall asleep, and sometimes it's so funny you could die from laughing.

When Angela came round to call for me on the Monday morning after half-term she was carrying a red cardboard folder.

'Hi, Charlie,' she said, when I let her in the kitchen door. 'I've brought my story for you to check over. Seeing as how you're such an expert.'

The way she said expert made it sound like some sort of a disease. It's not my fault if I'm good at writing stories and always come top in Composition, but Angela is never pleased when Miss Bridge gives me stars for my work. So the week before, when I got two gold stars for my story called 'The Magic Wellingtons', Angela was really mad at me and didn't speak to me for the rest of the day.

I shut the kitchen door behind her and went back to the table.

'I'm still eating my breakfast,' I said, buttering my third slice of toast and opening a new jar of my mum's home-made blackberry jelly. 'But you can read it to me if you like. I'll tell you if there are any mistakes.'

Angela sat down opposite me with her elbows on the kitchen table.

'It's called "A Winter's Night",' she began, in her best posh newsreader's voice. '"It was a cold, dark night in December. The night watch-

man watched the icy wind blowing the snowflakes along the gutter. Pulling his threadbare
cloak closer about his thin shoulders, he
reached out to warm his numb hands upon his
glowing brazzier . . .'''

Angela's voice trailed off because I was
nearly choking on my mouthful of toast and
jam. She jumped up and banged me on the
back until I finally managed to stop splutter-
ing. Then I wiped my streaming eyes on my
hanky.

'Sorry,' I gasped. 'Swallowed a crumb.
What were you saying? Warmed his hands on
his what?'

'His brazzier,' said Angela patiently. 'You
know, one of those little furnace things, with
coal and stuff on. They used to roast chestnuts
on them in the olden days.'

I carefully swallowed the last of my tea and
carried the cup over to the sink. I had to keep
my back to Angela so that she wouldn't see
my face.

'Oh, yes,' I said. 'I know what you mean.
Go on with the story.'

Well, I know I should have told her she

wasn't saying it right. But I couldn't help thinking about all the times she's done horrible things to me, like pouring glue all down the front of my party dress because it was nicer than hers, and this seemed like a good chance to get my own back for a change. So I kept my mouth shut about her mistake, and when she had finished the story I clapped and cheered as if it was the Muppet Show.

'Not bad at all,' I said. 'Put in a few full stops here and there and it'll be worth at least two gold stars.'

Angela's face went pink. 'Do you think so?' she said, sounding all pleased with herself. 'I hope Miss Bridge thinks so, too.'

My mum came into the kitchen just then with her arms full of dirty clothes for the washing machine.

'It's twenty to nine, girls,' she said. 'You two had better get a move on or you'll be late for school.'

She shooed us out of the door and we had to run all the way. The first day back after half-term is always good fun, because everybody has such a lot to talk about and even the teachers don't seem quite as weary and dreary as usual. We spent the morning settling back to work, and I didn't have time to think about Angela's story at all.

Then the afternoon came. Miss Bridge carried her big chair from behind her desk and placed it in front of the class.

'Story Time, everybody,' she said, her face all smiles, and I bet she only invented it so she could take it easy and have a nice rest every Monday afternoon. 'I believe it's Angela Mitchell's story we're going to hear today.'

Angela walked out to the front of the class with her red folder. She looked all smug and pleased with herself and I got that nasty sinking feeling in my stomach that you get when the dentist tells you how many fillings you need. I wished like anything that I'd explained to her about braziers and brassières. But it was too late now.

Angela sat down in Miss Bridge's chair and opened her folder. She cleared her throat importantly as if she was going to read the news on telly. Miss Bridge perched on a stool at the back of the room and everybody settled down to listen.

'"A Winter's Night",' announced Angela, loudly and clearly. '"It was a cold, dark night in December. The night watchman watched the icy wind blowing the snowflakes along the gutter. Pulling his threadbare cloak closer about his thin shoulders, he reached out to warm his numb hands upon his glowing brazzier . . ."'

Laurence Parker was the first to burst out sniggering, and Angela's voice faltered and then stopped altogether. I could see everybody raising their eyebrows and grinning and nudging one another, and in no time at all we were all hooting with laughter and even Miss Bridge hid a smile behind her hanky.

And of course I was laughing just as much as anybody, even though I felt mean about the whole thing. Angela looked all red and baffled and furious, and I felt sure she wouldn't speak to me ever again.

Miss Bridge walked out to the blackboard and held up her hand for silence. When the noise had died down a bit she took a piece of chalk and wrote the word *brazier* on the board.

'That's what you mean, is it, Angela?' she said.

'Yes, Miss Bridge,' muttered Angela, hanging her head and sulking. 'It's a sort of fire.'

'That's quite right,' said Miss Bridge kindly. 'But we pronounce it *bray-zier*. A *brassière* is an article of, er . . . ladies' underwear.'

And that set everybody off all over again. Isn't it funny the way people always laugh whenever anybody mentions underwear? You can say swimsuit or dungarees or pullover and nobody bats an eyelid. But you try saying knickers and see what happens. Comedians do it all the time on the telly. And my mum tuts and sniffs and says it's a pity that's the only way they can make their audience laugh and it's only fools who find it funny anyway. And my dad stops laughing and says he quite agrees.

Miss Bridge soon stopped the giggles with one of her fierce looks.

'That's quite enough,' she said sternly. 'We'll hear the rest of Angela's story now, and there's to be no more of this silliness. It's very bad manners to laugh at other people's mistakes.'

So Angela finished reading her story and when it was over we all clapped politely and Miss Bridge gave her a gold star. In fact, Miss Bridge was nice to her for the rest of the afternoon. She even let her fetch her cup of tea from the staff room at break time, although it should really have been my turn.

When lessons were over for the day and we were all trooping down the corridor to the cloakroom, Angela caught up with me and tucked her arm through mine.

'Be as quick as you can, Charlie,' she hissed in my ear. 'I've got something special to tell you.'

I stared at her and she winked. She wasn't mad at me at all, and I could hardly believe it. I was so pleased and astonished that I changed my shoes and collected my things from my peg as fast as I could. She was waiting for me in the playground when I came out and as soon as she saw me she grabbed hold of my hand.

'Hurry up, slowcoach!' she said. 'We've got to get there first.' And she began to pull me away from the school buildings, down the gravel path by the playing field, and all the way to the games shed at the bottom.

'Where are we going?' I panted, out of breath. 'What are you up to now?'

She didn't bother to answer. She kept on dragging me along until we rounded the corner of the shed, then she pulled me down on the grass behind it.

The games shed is an old wooden shack in the corner of the playing field. It's where we keep all the stuff for sports lessons, bats and balls and hoops and mats and all sorts of things like that. The door is kept locked, and the place is out of bounds after school.

'We're not allowed down here after school,' I said, when I'd got my breath back. 'We'll get into trouble.' I didn't like the look in her eyes, and I liked it even less when she fished a key out of her blazer pocket and dangled it in front of my face.

'What's that?' I said stupidly.

'The games shed key, of course,' said Angela,

grinning all over her face. 'I pinched it from the staff room at break time.' She jumped to her feet and did a little dance on the grass. 'We're going to lock up that fat fool, Laurence Parker. That'll teach him to snigger at my stories.'

She disappeared round the corner and I could hear her unlocking the shed door. I sat there and chewed my nails, wondering what I could do to stop her.

She flopped down beside me and looked at her watch.

'He'll be here in a minute,' she said, hugging herself with glee. 'I sent him a note. I told him to meet me in the shed to share my box of Smarties. You know what a pig he is.'

'He won't come,' I said hopefully. 'He knows you hate him. He'll suspect it's a trick.'

'I thought of that,' said Angela with a giggle. 'I didn't sign my name on the note. I signed yours.'

I was flabbergasted, I can tell you.

'You WHAT?' I said. 'You rotten . . .' She quickly put her hand over my mouth to shut me up because just then we heard footsteps crunching on the gravel path.

'That's him!' whispered Angela excitedly.

We clung together and held our breaths as the footsteps drew nearer. We heard the shed door creak open and somebody moving about inside.

'Now!' hissed Angela, leaping to her feet.

We dashed round the corner and I slammed the door shut while Angela quickly turned the key in the lock. Then we grabbed our satchels and books and fled. And it was awful because the banging and shouting and cries for help followed us halfway up the field. But by the time we reached the school buildings the sounds had become so faint you had to listen very hard to hear them at all. And in any case everybody had gone home except Mr Edwards, the caretaker, and he's as deaf as a door.

We slowed to a walking pace when we were halfway home. Angela was giggling all the way, but I couldn't help feeling more than a bit sorry for poor old Laurence Parker and I wondered what his mother would think when he didn't come home from school. I wished like anything that I hadn't helped lock him up, and I hoped Angela would go back and let him out soon.

But when I suggested it she only laughed harder than ever. And then when we got home she pushed the games shed key into my hand.

'What's that for?' I said. I stared down at it and I suddenly had a nasty feeling in my bones.

'You'll have to let him out,' she said. 'I won't have time. We're going to my cousin Dominic's for tea.'

I gazed at her in horror but I got no chance to argue. Angela's gate suddenly opened and there was Auntie Sally, tut-tutting like anything at Angela for being late and whisking her away in the yellow Mini. Angela grinned and waved at me from the back window as they shot off down the street, and I really think she expected me to wave back.

I put the key in my pocket and went into the house. There was a lovely smell because my mum had been baking, but even warm scones and strawberry jam and cream couldn't cheer me up. I sat at the table and slowly stirred my tea round and round. Laurence Parker would murder me, I felt sure. And the longer I left him the madder he would be.

My mum could see that something was wrong.

'What's up, Charlie?' she said. 'You've hardly touched your tea. Aren't you feeling very well?'

'I'm all right,' I said, not feeling all right at all. 'I'm just not very hungry at the moment. Can I go out for a while, and save my tea till later?'

'Yes, if you like,' said my mum. 'But I can't promise there'll be any scones left when you get back. Not if your dad arrives home first.'

So I pulled on my old green anorak and set off down the street. At first I walked quite quickly, but as I drew nearer the school I got slower and slower, like a clockwork mouse that needs winding up. I sat down on the library steps for a while to wait for my courage to come back.

'Hi, Charlie,' said a voice behind me suddenly. 'What are you sitting there for?'

I looked up and there he was. Laurence

Parker. As large as life and fat as ever. Coming down the library steps with his arms full of books. And I used to think it was only in stories that people's eyes popped out of their heads but that's what mine were doing all right.

'How . . . what . . . how did you get out?' I managed to stammer.

'Get out?' said Laurence. 'Get out of where?' Then he gave a whoop of laughter. 'I get it! You were going to lock me up, were you. I bet it was your friend Angela's idea. Well, it didn't work, so there!' And he walked away up the road, sniggering and making rude faces over his shoulder as he went.

And I sat there with my stomach full of lead. Angela and I had locked somebody up in the shed. If it wasn't Laurence Parker, who could it have been?

He turned round at the corner beside the butcher's shop.

'If you're wondering what happened to the note,' he shouted. 'I guessed it was a trick. I gave it to Miss Bridge!'

I don't know how I did it but I did. I ran

all the way up the road to the school and down the path to the shed and I think opening that door was the bravest thing I ever did in my whole life and I was so scared my fingers couldn't turn the key in the lock but at last I got it open. And there was Miss Bridge, with cobwebs in her hair and her face all red and smeared with dust and a hole in her tights from trying to climb out of the tiny window. She looked as though she could have murdered me, and I think it was a miracle that she didn't.

And so that was how I got one of the worst telling-offs I ever had. She wasn't a bit grateful to be let out, and she screamed and shouted at me for hours even though her voice was already a bit hoarse from calling for help. And all I could do was stand there looking sorry for myself, because I couldn't say anything about Angela's share of the blame. She wouldn't have believed me anyway. Not when it was my name on the note.

Then Miss Bridge calmed down a bit and let me go, saying she would report me to Miss Collingwood on Monday, which meant another telling-off, and giving me a rotten old essay to write as a punishment. So I had to spend the whole evening writing about 'Why I must not play silly and dangerous pranks', instead of watching *Neighbours* on the telly. And to crown it all when I got home my dad had eaten all the scones. Life does seem a bit unfair, sometimes.

I t was in the middle of the summer holidays
when Angela and I found that nice little
brown puppy in the woods, and it turned out to
be one of those awful mistakes that make you
go all cold when you think about it afterwards.

I was planning to help my dad to weed his
rows of onions in the vegetable patch, but
Angela turned up at the back door just as I was
going outside in my oldest teeshirt and shorts.

'Come on, Charlie,' she said. 'We're going
for a picnic.'

Angela had her new green cotton jumpsuit on and her hair was tied back in a green ribbon. She looked lovely. She was carrying a basket with a white cloth over it.

'I can't,' I said. 'I'm much too busy. I've got to help my dad in the garden.' I've been on picnics with Angela before, and something terrible always happens.

Angela scowled. 'I've spent hours packing this great basket with stuff,' she said crossly. 'I thought it would be a nice surprise for you. Look, there's ham sandwiches and sausage rolls and smoky bacon crisps and chocolate cake and a tin of peaches. What am I supposed to do with all that?'

My stomach rumbled and it seemed a long time since breakfast.

'Well . . .' I said weakly. 'I did sort of promise my dad.'

'But it's the holidays,' objected Angela. 'You don't have to work when it's the holidays. Does she, Uncle Ted?' she said to my dad, who was just coming out of the toolshed with a trowel in his hand.

'What?' he said. 'No, of course she doesn't.

Not if there's something else she wants to do instead.' He gave me a smile. 'Off you go and enjoy yourself, sweetheart,' he said. 'You can help me another time.'

I looked from Angela to my dad and then back again, and I didn't know what to do. Angela lifted the corner of the cloth and waved the basket under my nose.

'Oh, all right, I'll come,' I said. 'But we'll only stay away a little while. Then I can help my dad this afternoon.'

Angela and I carried the basket between us and set off towards the woods near the river. We passed Lunnon's Farm and walked along the edge of the gravel pit lake, and before long I started to feel very glad I came because it was warm and sunny and the birds were singing and Angela was in a good mood after getting her own way.

We wandered into the woods, looking around for a good place to have our picnic. And after a while we found the perfect spot, a fallen tree trunk in a sunny clearing. We sat astride it facing one another while Angela unpacked the basket and spread out the cloth between us. I don't know why it is that food always tastes so good in the open air, but everything was delicious. And if you've never eaten sliced peaches straight out of the tin with your fingers, with the juice trickling down your wrist, you don't know what you've been missing.

'Do you want to finish the last sausage roll, Charlie?' said Angela, starting to put the paper bags and wrappers back into the basket. I heaved a great big sigh.

'I haven't got room,' I groaned. 'I can hardly move. That chocolate cake was yummy.'

'My mum made it,' said Angela, looking all smug.

We flopped down on a patch of grass in the sunshine to let our lunch settle down a bit and it was all quiet and still and sort of peaceful with just the odd twittering of a bird. I lay on my stomach and watched a tiny blue and green beetle climbing up a blade of grass. Soon I began to feel sleepy. And that's when we heard the faint whimpering noise coming from somewhere nearby.

'What was that?' I said, sitting up suddenly.

Angela had heard it too, and was already on her feet.

'Sounds like an animal,' she said. 'Let's see if we can find it.'

We hunted about among the ferns and brambles, following the whimpering sound, and it was in a big clump of bracken beside the old fence that we found the puppy. His hind legs were caught up in a nasty tangle of rusty barbed wire, and he was struggling to get free. Every now and then he gave a weak little cry, and it was a good job he did, or we would never have found him.

'It's a little puppy,' said Angela, kneeling down beside him. 'The poor thing. He's all in a tangle.' But as soon as she put her hands out towards him, the puppy began to hiss and spit. More like a kitten than a dog.

'There, there,' said Angela soothingly. 'We're only trying to help you. And you needn't stand there looking stupid, Charlie Ellis. Come and give me a hand.'

Well, it wasn't a bit easy getting him untangled, I can tell you. Especially as he kept wriggling about and trying to bite us all the time. The wire was old and stiff and I got one or two bad scratches from it, as well as plenty of nips from the puppy's sharp little teeth. But at last we managed to get him free. Angela carried him over to our tree and plonked him down on the table-cloth so we could have a good look at him.

I fell in love with him at once. He really was the nicest puppy I had ever seen. His coat was dark brown, with a paler brown on his chest and tummy, and he had a cute little pointed face and a thick bushy tail. He looked a bit thin, and he had a few nasty scratches on his back legs from the wire, but otherwise he seemed very healthy.

He had already made up his mind that he didn't like us at all. He was still growling in the back of his throat and spitting in that funny way of his, and if Angela hadn't kept a good grip on the scruff of his neck he would have jumped off that log and run away.

'He's probably starving,' I said. 'Let's give him that last sausage roll.' I fished it out of the basket and put it on the cloth beside the puppy, and I've never seen a sausage roll disappear so fast in my life. Except when my dad pinches one hot from the baking tray when my mum isn't looking.

The puppy licked up every crumb and then started sniffing round for more.

'He's ravishing with hunger,' said Angela.

'Ravenous,' I said.

'Yes,' said Angela. 'That's what I said. He could have been here for days. I think we'd better take him home and give him a good meal.'

The sausage roll must have convinced the puppy we were friends, because he didn't seem to mind when I picked him up and put him in the basket. He was soon having a fine old time tearing up paper bags and sniffing out the last few specks of food. I held the basket in my arms while Angela tidied up the picnic place and scraped a hole in the earth with the tin-opener to bury the empty peach tin. She folded up the cloth and put it in the basket with the puppy.

Then off we went home. We chatted all the way about who the puppy might belong to, and why they hadn't come to look for him, and how long he had been trapped in the woods, and what we were going to do with him, and that's what started the argument.

'I can't take him home, stupid!' said Angela, sounding all horrified. 'You know my mum won't have a dog in the house any more. Not after the last one.'

Angela used to have a lovely big dog called King, but he turned all nasty and bad-tempered and they had to give him away after he bit Angela on the ankle. If you ask me it was because Angela was always being mean and horrible and teasing him all the time. I know just how he must have felt. I feel like biting her on the ankle myself, sometimes.

'We'd better take him straight to the police station,' said Angela. 'They'll know what to do.' My heart sank.

I looked down into the basket. The puppy had got tired of chewing everything in sight and was now fast asleep, tucked up under the picnic cloth like a sausage in a toad-in-the-hole.

'No,' I said. 'They'll only shut him up in a

nasty concrete cage. And then if he isn't claimed they'll take him away and have him put to sleep. We've got to think of something else.'

But by the time we reached my gate we still hadn't thought of anything.

'You'll just have to put him in your play-shed,' said Angela. 'Just until we decide what to do. I'll come round later and we'll have a special meeting and take a vote.'

I knew it wouldn't do any good. Angela's idea of a special meeting is for her to be the chairman and for her vote to count as two. But there was no time to argue. My mum was waving at me from the living room window and I had to hide the puppy before she spotted him.

The playshed is a good place to hide things because nobody goes in there unless they're invited by me. Except Angela of course who always barges in as if she owned the place. So when I shut the puppy in there, I knew there was no chance of my mum or dad finding him by accident. I weeded the rows of onions and shallots in the vegetable garden for the rest of the afternoon, and then after tea I hurried back down to the shed with half a beefburger that I'd managed to smuggle into my pocket.

You should have seen how pleased that little dog was to see me. Especially when I gave him the bit of beefburger. But what a mess he had made. All my books and papers were pulled down off the shelves and scattered over the floor. The rubbish bin had been overturned and there were bits of chewed paper everywhere. And that wasn't all. There was a big damp patch, right in the middle of my furry rug.

I knew it was my own fault, because I hadn't left him any sort of toilet tray, and I was busy scooping some dry soil into an old washing-up bowl when Angela arrived.

'What's that for?' she asked, following me back into the shed.

'It's Bruno's loo,' I told her, putting it on the floor in the corner.

'Bruno?' she said. 'Why Bruno?'

'Because he's got a brown coat,' I said. 'Bruno means brown.'

'So it does,' said Angela admiringly. 'You're

not as stupid as you look, Charlie Ellis.' She knelt down to pat the puppy. 'Come on, Bruno. See what I've brought for you.'

And I could have hugged her, because she'd been all the way down to the supermarket and spent the last of her pocket money on a big tin of Meaty Chunks. We still had the picnic tin-opener, and it wasn't long before Bruno was tucking in to a proper dinner at last.

And of course we never did have a special meeting, after all. We just played with Bruno all evening until it got dark, and when it was time for bed we still hadn't decided what to do about him.

'We'll think about it tomorrow,' I said, as Angela was leaving. 'Or maybe the day after.' And Angela grinned at me, because she knew I was only putting it off.

I had wanted a dog of my own all my life, as long as I could remember. So you can guess what it felt like to have a puppy like Bruno to look after, even though I knew it could only be for a little while. Day after day went by, and the longer I kept him the harder it was to think about giving him up. And in the end we kept that poor animal locked up in the shed for three whole weeks.

I don't know how we did it without being found out. Being the holidays helped, because we could spend a lot of time playing with him and keeping him amused. I was allowed to eat a lot of my meals out of doors, which made it easy to save scraps of food, and we spent nearly all our pocket money on tins of dog food as well.

We did have one or two nasty moments, though. Like the time I was shopping in the supermarket with my mum.

'No Meaty Chunks today?' asked the assistant, giving me a friendly smile.

'Er . . . no,' I mumbled. 'I've, er . . . gone off it.'

My face went scarlet and the assistant gave me such a funny look and it was lucky my mum was so busy sorting out her change or we would have been found out there and then.

Bruno was now growing fast and I was beginning to worry that he wasn't getting enough exercise. Especially as he was now doing his best to get out of the shed every time

I left him there. The door and the window-frame were all bitten and scratched where he had tried to escape.

Something else was bothering me, too. Bruno wasn't a bit like any dog I had ever known. He never barked or yapped for a start. And his dark brown coat was slowly changing colour and turning a lovely rusty red. His tail had thickened out and turned white at the tip, and his narrow little face looked sharper than ever. I had a horrible feeling in my bones that Angela and I had made a terrible mistake.

And then one evening during a spell of hot, sunny weather, Bruno and I were playing his favourite romping game together in the shed when Angela walked in.

'Pooh!' she said, holding her nose as soon as she was in the door. 'It doesn't half stink in here. How much longer are you going to keep this poor animal locked up?'

I had to admit to myself that the shed was starting to pong a bit. Bruno was very good about using his tray, and I changed the soil every morning, but what with the warm weather and having to keep the door and window shut all the time, you can imagine it didn't smell very nice.

'I can't smell anything,' I said stubbornly, scratching Bruno's head between his ears.

'Rubbish!' snorted Angela. 'It's horrible in here. It's time he got some fresh air and proper exercise. We ought to take him out for a walk.'

I nearly had a fit. 'We can't,' I said quickly. 'We'll get into trouble. Somebody will see us.'

'No they won't,' said Angela. 'We'll sneak out at dead of night. It'll be a super adventure.'

I didn't like the idea a bit. But I knew Angela was right about Bruno needing exercise, and in the end I gave in.

So that night, when everybody was fast asleep and the hands on my Mickey Mouse clock said half-past twelve, I slipped out of bed. I put on my dark jeans and a black polo-necked sweater, and my old plimsolls so I wouldn't make a noise. I put a small torch in my pocket and sneaked down the stairs and out of the back door.

Angela was already in the playshed, fastening a bit of rope around Bruno's neck in the

dark. Bruno was leaping about with excitement and I had to hold him still before we
could get the rope tied properly. We managed
it at last, and then off we went down the drive
into the street.

We had a heck of a job hanging on to him,
I can tell you. It took all our strength to hold
the rope, and even then he towed us along like
a husky with an eskimo sledge. We raced along
behind him, getting more and more out of
breath, and it was when we reached the lane
leading down to Lunnon's Farm that the awful
thing happened. The thing I'd been dreading
ever since we set off. Bruno stopped dead with
his nose raised as though sniffing the air. Then,
suddenly and unexpectedly, he took off again
like a rocket. The rope slipped through our
fingers and he was free, dashing off through
the trees towards the farm buildings.

I don't often swear but I said the very
rudest word I could think of.

'Don't just stand there!' shouted Angela.
'Let's get after him!'

We plunged into the woods, but although
we searched and searched, blundering about

in the nettles and brambles for hours and hours, there was still no sign of Bruno anywhere. I had to keep swallowing hard and blinking back the tears as we plodded off home in the early morning light, and I crawled back into bed with a great nasty stone in my chest where my heart should have been. I was sure I would never see Bruno again.

I was wrong.

I slept late the next morning because of roaming around half the night and it was just after nine o'clock when my dad came banging on my bedroom door.

'I think you'd better get up, Charlie,' he said, sticking his head in. 'Mr Lunnon wants a word with you. And so do I, for that matter,' he added grimly.

He looked so cross that I didn't dare ask him what was going on. I pulled on some clothes as slowly as I could but I couldn't put off going downstairs much longer.

'Let nothing bad have happened,' I muttered over and over again, as I walked down the hall to the kitchen.

I stood on the threshold and looked in and

there was Farmer Lunnon, so tall that his head almost touched the ceiling, wearing his greeny-brown tweed jacket with the leather patches on the elbows. In one hand he was holding a big mug of tea. And in the other he was holding a bit of rope with a small reddish dog tied to it. My dog, Bruno.

I stared and stared and it was then I knew I couldn't kid myself any longer. Bruno wasn't a dog at all. And of course I must have really known it all along. I just hadn't wanted to believe it. I gazed at the floor and shuffled my feet.

'Hello, Charlie,' said Farmer Lunnon. 'Do you know anything about this young fox, by any chance?'

It wouldn't have done the slightest bit of good to deny it. Bruno suddenly looked up and saw me and launched himself at me with little yelps of delight. He leaped about and tried to lick my face and he wouldn't settle down until I knelt beside him and put my arms around his neck.

And so, bit by bit, I told them the whole story. All about finding Bruno trapped in the woods and thinking he was just an ordinary puppy and keeping him in the shed all that time so the police wouldn't put him to sleep and spending all my pocket money on tins of food. And the grown-ups drank their tea and listened quietly and looked at one another and shook their heads and tut-tutted in the way that only grown-ups can.

'And then when we got to the farm he got away from us,' I finished miserably. 'We looked and looked but we couldn't find him. So we came home.'

There was a short silence while they all looked at me. Then Farmer Lunnon cleared his throat.

'He must have smelled the hens, Charlie,' he said. 'That's where I found him this morning. Chasing them up and down the run and creating a proper din, he was. Feathers everywhere, there were, but none of the hens was hurt, I'm glad to say. You're lucky I didn't shoot him.'

The farmer swallowed the last of his tea and put the mug on the kitchen table. 'I noticed the rope around his neck,' he said. 'So I chased

91

him up the lane and followed him home. He led me all the way to your garden shed. You won't be able to keep him, you know, Charlie.'

And that's when I started to cry. I couldn't help it. I put my face against Bruno's neck and sobbed and sobbed. And it was awful because the more they tried to comfort me the louder I howled and when my dad came and put his arms round me it only made me worse.

It all got sorted out in the end and it wasn't too bad, I suppose. After a lot of arguing the grown-ups decided we couldn't release Bruno back to the wild now that he was so tame, and Mr Lunnon said he knew of a wild-life reserve where there was already a family of foxes.

And so that's where they took him. It's a bit like a safari park, and I can go and see him as often as I like. It's not the same as keeping him myself, but it's better than not seeing him at all.

And it's not all rubbish what they say about clouds and silver linings, because on my next birthday my dad is going to buy me my very own dog. My mum has agreed to put up with hairs on the carpet, providing I help with the vacuuming now and again. I might even train it to bite Angela's ankles whenever she's nasty to me. It would serve her right.

7

We were eating breakfast in the kitchen one Saturday morning, and I felt sorry for my dad because he was only having a cup of lemon tea and half a grapefruit without sugar. My mum had finally made him go on a diet, and you should have heard the moans and groans. Especially when he saw what my mum and I were eating. Sausages and fried bread and tomatoes.

'It's not fair,' he said faintly, looking longingly at our plates. 'How can you sit there stuffing yourselves with that lot while I starve to death?' And he hid his face behind the newspaper so he wouldn't have to watch.

'It's very rude to read the paper at the table,' said my mum crossly. 'What's in it that's so interesting, anyway?'

My dad laid the paper down with a sigh.

'Not a lot,' he said. 'The Cookburn Green Jazz Band is looking for a new double bass.' He started scraping out the last drops of grapefruit juice with his spoon, and my mum winked at me.

'Why don't you apply for the job?' she asked him with a grin. 'You're about the right shape and size.'

'All right, all right. Very funny, I'm sure,' said my dad, while my mum and I giggled together. But I don't really mind my dad being a bit fat. It makes him more cuddly, like a teddy bear. It's only my mum who keeps going on about how fit and slim Uncle Jim is, with all his tennis and squash and stuff, while the only exercise my dad gets is lifting his pint of beer and switching channels on the telly.

When we'd finished breakfast my mum got up and began to clear the table.

'Come on, you two,' she said briskly. 'I want you both out of my kitchen today. I'm helping Sally with the food for tomorrow's christening party.'

Angela's baby cousin, Sarah Jane, was being christened the next day, at the same church in Edgebourne where Auntie Beth had been christened herself. The tea party was at Angela's house because they've got a lot of room there. And loads of people had been invited, including me.

'We'd better clear off for the day, Charlie,' said my dad, getting up from the table. 'How about a drive up to Birmingham to see Welly? We haven't seen him for ages.'

Welly is an old army friend of my dad's and his real name is Mr. Welton. He keeps a sort of rest home for retired horses a few miles from Birmingham, and I always like to visit him and see all the nice old donkeys and ponies enjoying themselves in the fields.

'Oh, goody,' I said. 'We'll take lots of sugar lumps and carrots for the horses and we'll stop for lunch at that nice snack bar where we stopped the last time and I'll wear my new red coat and my new brown shoes that I got for the christening and I'll sit in the front seat of the car and we'll . . .'

'Hold on, hold on,' interrupted my mum. 'You'll wear your old dungarees and your green anorak and your plimsolls and no arguments. I'm not having smelly old horses wiping their noses on your nice new coat. I want you looking respectable in church tomorrow, young lady.'

I knew it wouldn't do any good to argue, so I just made a face behind her back and then ran off upstairs to change. While I was in my room I heard a knock at the back door, and when I came down again I found Angela in the kitchen talking to my dad.

'I'd better go and ask my mum,' she was saying. 'But I'm sure it'll be all right. Hi, Charlie. I'll be back in a minute.' And off she went.

'I've asked Angela to come with us,' said my dad. 'She'll be company for you while I have a good natter with Welly about old times. OK?'

'Yes, fine,' I said, not knowing whether it was or not. I had been looking forward to having my dad all to myself for a while, but on the other hand I did want Angela to see the lovely horses and show off to her that I knew all their names.

My dad and I did the washing-up together while we waited for Angela to come back, and after about ten minutes she appeared. She looked all smart in her pale pink leggings and a darker pink tunic top and black suede boots with the sort of heels my mum won't let me have because they're too grown up. She looked me up and down, and I could see she wasn't impressed by my old dungarees and my grubby anorak.

'Hurry up and get ready, Charlie,' she said.

'I am ready,' I said, feeling like a refugee. 'Those good clothes will get ever so dirty, mind.'

'So what?' said Angela, tossing back her long hair. 'They can be washed, can't they?'

There was no answer to that, so I started helping my dad put some apples and carrots and a few handfuls of sugar lumps into a plastic bag. Then we were ready to go, and my mum came outside with us to see us off. I climbed into the front passenger seat of our old Morris. But Angela was standing in the drive smiling sweetly up at my dad.

'I'll have to sit in the front, I'm afraid, Uncle Ted,' she said. 'I'll get travel sickness if I sit in the back.'

'OK,' he said. 'I'm sure Charlie doesn't mind.'

I did mind. I minded like anything. And I could have kicked her because it was a downright fib. She's never been car sick in her life, and she only likes to sit in the front to get the best view. But I got out and climbed in the back without saying a word. She's quite capable of being sick on purpose if she doesn't get her own way.

At last we were off. The car rolled down the drive and my mum stood on the doorstep and waved.

'Keep an eye on your dad, Charlie,' she called. 'Don't let him eat chips and stuff. He's only allowed fruit for lunch.' And it wasn't half a good job my mum couldn't hear what my dad said under his breath about that.

I soon forgot to sulk as we drove through the sunny lanes. Dad kept away from the busy motorways and stuck to winding little country roads, and we sang silly songs and told each other jokes as we went along. I told them about Uncle Barrie's latest funny poem.

'There was a young lady from Ickenham
Who went on a bus-trip to Twickenham
She drank too much beer
Which made her feel queer
So she took off her boots and was sick in 'em.'

And I think we all got just a little bit too silly and high-spirited, because we were in a crazy sort of mood by the time we stopped for lunch at the café on the outskirts of Birmingham.

'What about hamburgers and chips and milk shakes, girls?' said my dad as he parked the car, and it sounded like a very good idea.

'Not for you, though, Uncle Ted,' said Angela. 'You can only have fruit.'

My dad groaned.

'I'm sick to death of fruit,' he said. 'Fruit for breakfast. Fruit for lunch. Fruit for supper. I'll be looking like a blooming monkey if this goes on much longer.' And with a loud whooping cry he began to lope along through the car-park with his jaw stuck out and his arms swinging in front of him like a chimpanzee.

Angela and I were helpless with giggles. We chased my dad round and round the car-park, and at last we pushed him through the café doorway and into the food queue, where he stood puffing and grinning.

'Come on, Charlie. We'll bag a table,' said Angela, and we looked round the crowded room. The place was packed with people, all eating chips and cream cakes and stuff and drinking tea and coffee and talking at the tops of their voices and clattering their knives and forks. At first we couldn't see any empty seats at all, but Angela spotted a table near the wall and pulled me towards it.

There were three spare chairs at the table. The fourth was occupied by an enormously fat lady eating cream doughnuts. Heaps of packages and shopping bags lay all around her, piled up on the table and taking up most of the space under it as well.

'We'll never squeeze in there,' I muttered into Angela's ear. 'That woman's taking all the room.'

'I think I know how to get rid of her,' whispered Angela, and she had that glint in her eye that always means she's up to no good.

We sat down on two of the chairs and Angela gave the fat lady one of her most angelic smiles. The fat lady smiled back through a mouthful of cream and jam.

'I hope you don't mind us sharing your table,' said Angela. 'But my friend's a bit upset.'

I was still wiping my eyes and blowing my nose from all the laughing, and the fat lady stared at me curiously.

'What's the matter?' she asked.

Angela at once put on her tragic face. She looked round quickly to make sure no one else was listening, then she leaned towards the fat lady's ear.

'She's upset about her dad,' she said in a hoarse, dramatic whisper. 'She thought he was getting better, but he's getting worse.'

The fat lady's eyes grew round and she forgot all about the cake she was eating.

'That's awful,' she breathed. 'What's wrong with him? He isn't going to . . .?'

Angela shook her head sadly and tapped herself on the forehead.

'It's his mind,' she said solemnly, kicking my shin under the table when she saw I was going to argue. 'He's been funny ever since he came back from the African jungle. Now they have to keep him in a mental hospital.'

The fat lady gasped and her eyes swivelled round to me.

'The poor child!' she said. 'Does she never see him?'

'Oh, yes,' said Angela. 'They let him out at weekends. Here he comes now.' And she waved at my dad who was coming towards us with a loaded tray.

'It's all right, he's not dangerous,' Angela told the fat lady quickly. 'He only thinks he's a chimpanzee.'

The fat lady's mouth fell open and she watched in shocked silence as my dad unloaded the three plates of food. He put hamburgers and chips and strawberry milk shakes in front of Angela and me and we all fixed our eyes on the third plate. My dad's diet lunch. Two small bananas.

Angela patted my dad's arm sympathetically.

'Monkey food again, Uncle Ted?' she said. And I nearly died, because my dad began to hop from one foot to the other and make gibbering noises and beat his chest with his fists and scratch under his armpits and wave his bananas in the air right there in front of all those people.

There was a sudden loud clatter as the fat lady leapt out of her chair, snatched up all her packages and shopping bags and rushed towards the door as fast as her legs would carry her.

My dad gazed after her in dismay.

'Oh, dear,' he said. 'She doesn't like my sense of humour.'

'Perhaps she just doesn't like monkeys,' said Angela, and we collapsed with the giggles all over again.

So that was how Angela managed to get us

a table to ourselves. And it was so funny seeing that enormous lady scuttling away in such a hurry that I forgot to be mad at Angela for saying those things about my dad. Especially when my dad thought it was so hilarious. And when we finally got to Welly's house and my dad told him all about it, he thought it was hilarious, too.

I'm glad my mum wasn't there, though. She wouldn't have thought it was funny at all. Making an exhibition of ourselves, she would have called it. I wonder if it's always the dads who are the wild and naughty ones and the mums who are the sensible ones. Or is it sometimes the other way round?

But I soon stopped worrying about it, because Angela and I had a great time playing with the ponies, and I had to laugh when she got her pink tunic sleeve chewed by a donkey. Welly gave us tea at a little table outside the cottage door in the sunshine, and there were fresh strawberries straight from his garden. And my dad made Angela and me promise that we wouldn't tell my mum about the great dollop of cream he had on his.

8

We were just getting into the car to leave when the nicest thing of all happened.

'Blimey, I nearly forgot,' said Welly suddenly. 'Hang on a second. I've got something for Charlie.'

Welly disappeared into the cottage, and he was back in less than a minute, pushing a brown paper parcel through the back window into my lap.

'There you are, Charlie,' he said. 'Fiona left it for you last time she was home. It's not new, mind. It's just one she doesn't use any more.' He grinned at me through the open window. 'She thought you might like it, now that you're getting to be such a grown-up young lady.'

Fiona is Welly's daughter and she's twenty and she's a fashion model. You might have seen her on the telly advertising expensive perfume and stuff. She gets her picture in all the posh magazines, and she's always flying off to Bermuda and places like that to be photographed in fancy clothes. You should see how many pairs of shoes she's got. Even more than Auntie Sally and Angela put together, and that's saying something, I can tell you.

'Go on, then, Charlie,' said Angela impatiently. 'I'm dying to see what it is.' She hung over the back of her seat while I opened the parcel. Then we both said 'Ooh!' as I pulled out the nicest brown leather handbag you ever saw.

You could tell it was real leather by the soft glossy feel and that lovely leathery smell. There were lots of little flaps and pockets on it, and it had a strap that you could make short or long in case you wanted to wear it on your shoulder. The colour was a lovely dark brown, and I could see straight away that it was just the thing to go with my new shoes I'd got for the christening.

'Wow! It's super!' I said, and my voice came out all sort of squeaky. 'Thanks, Uncle Welly. I'll write to Fiona as soon as I get home.'

We all waved goodbye as we drove off and then I sat back in my seat, hugging my new bag in my arms like a baby. I was thinking how smart I was going to look in church tomorrow, and I didn't notice how quiet Angela was in the front. It was only afterwards that I realised she hadn't spoken a single word to anybody all the way home.

When the car stopped in our drive she got out and ignored me completely.

'Thank you very much, Uncle Ted,' she said, in that polite I-don't-really-mean-it sort of voice. 'I've had such a lovely time.' And she ran off home without saying goodbye.

I couldn't think what I could have done to

upset her. But I didn't let it bother me. I was too excited about my bag, and I couldn't wait to get indoors and show my mum.

And when she saw it she was just as thrilled as me.

'Good lord, it's a Gucci,' she said, looking at the label inside, and a look of awe came over her face. 'One of the very best designers. You'll have to take great care of it, Charlie. It must have been very expensive.'

There was a delicious ham salad waiting for us for supper, and afterwards I felt so tired from all the excitement that I went to bed early. I wrote a quick thank-you letter to Fiona, and then switched out the light. And the last thing I saw before I closed my eyes was the Gucci bag lying on the pillow beside me.

I was still in my pyjamas the next morning when my dad called up the stairs that Angela was on the phone. I ran down in my bare feet and picked up the receiver.

'Hello, Angela,' I said. 'It looks like a super day for the christening.'

'I didn't ring up to talk about the weather,'

said Angela, and her voice sounded so chilly and distant it made me want to shiver.

'It's about walking to church this afternoon,' she said. 'I said I'd be your partner, didn't I?'

Auntie Beth wanted us all to walk to church in a kind of procession, with the godmother carrying the baby in front. Angela and I had agreed to walk together at the end of the line.

'Yes, that's right,' I said. 'Why, what's up?'

There was a short silence and then I heard a sigh.

'Listen, Charlie, I don't want you to feel offended or anything. But I hope you're not thinking of bringing that old handbag your Uncle Welly gave you yesterday.'

At first I couldn't speak. I was so astonished I had to sit down on the little stool beside the telephone table. I remembered her face when I'd opened the parcel, and I could have sworn she liked the bag as much as I did.

'Well, er . . . yes, I was,' I managed to blurt out. 'Why? What's the matter with it?'

'Nothing,' said Angela quickly. 'Nothing at all. It's all right for somebody like you, I suppose. You bring it if you want to. But I wouldn't be seen dead with a tatty old-fashioned thing like that. And if you don't mind, I think I'll walk to church with my cousin Dominic.'

The phone went click and I sat there for ages just staring at the wall. After a while I went upstairs and sat on my bed with the handbag on my lap. I stroked the soft shiny leather and I sniffed its clean smell and I couldn't help wondering if Angela was right. Perhaps it was old-fashioned. Perhaps that was why Fiona didn't use it any more.

I had to make my own breakfast because my mum was dashing about between our kitchen and Auntie Sally's with last-minute trays of food for the christening tea. My dad was busy washing the car, so I took my bowl of cornflakes out into the sunshine and sat on the wooden bench under the apple tree.

But I felt so miserable I couldn't eat. I sat there fiddling with the spoon and gazing into space and that's where Angela found me a few minutes later. She sat down on the bench beside me and put her arm round my shoulders.

'Come on, Charlie. Cheer up,' she said. 'I'm sorry if I hurt your feelings. Here, I've brought you a present.' And she slid a large red plastic handbag into my lap.

'What's this?' I said stupidly. Angela giggled.

'It's a handbag,' she said. 'It's brand new. It's the one my grandma sent me from Blackpool last Christmas. And it's the exact same colour as your new coat.'

'It's plastic,' I said.

'Of course it's plastic,' said Angela patiently. 'It's modern and with-it and up-to-date and fashionable. Plastic is the *in thing* these days.' She gave my shoulder a push.

'Come on, silly,' she said. 'How many girls of our age do we know who have great big old-fashioned *secondhand* leather handbags like that? It's only fit for a jumble sale.'

I had to admit she was right. All the girls I know have coloured plastic handbags, if they have handbags at all. And Angela has always known better than me about what's in fashion and what isn't.

'All right,' I said, heaving a big sigh. 'What

shall I do? Borrow this red one for the christening?'

Angela jumped up at once.

'You can keep it,' she said, giving me a quick hug. 'It'll look super with your red coat. I'll take that old leather thing as a sort of swop. I dare say I'll be able to use it for something. Or give it to Oxfam, maybe.'

I scraped the soggy cornflakes out on to the bird table for the sparrows and we went indoors together. Angela pounced on the Gucci bag as soon as we were in my bedroom, and it was awful to see her walking off with it over her shoulder.

'No swoppies back, Charlie?' she said in the doorway, and I shook my head.

'No swoppies back,' I said. And we shook hands solemnly.

Now neither of us could change her mind about the swop, and Angela clattered away down the stairs, looking a bit like the cat that got the cream.

I didn't feel so bad about it that afternoon, though, when I got my new red coat out of the wardrobe and put it on. Angela was right.

The colour of the bag matched it exactly, and I felt smart as anything when I came downstairs to tell my mum and dad I was ready. My dad hugged me tight and said I was the bee's knees, and he didn't say a word about the handbag although he gave it a bit of a funny look.

My mum was too busy to notice me much, and she hardly had time to get ready herself. But at last she put on her new straw hat and we all walked round to Angela's house to join the others.

We found a crowd of people on the patio, all wearing their best clothes and standing about chatting and drinking glasses of sherry. Auntie Sally was holding the baby, who looked ever so sweet in her white robe and the lacy christening shawl that's been in their family for about a hundred years. I looked around for my friend Angela, and that's when I got a very nasty shock.

There she was, looking prettier than ever, and showing off as usual. She was wearing a long-sleeved dress of fine cream wool with a brown collar and cuffs and a matching brown belt. Her long blonde hair was brushed out loose, and she had a lovely cream straw hat with a brown silk band. Her cream lacy tights exactly matched the colour of her dress. And her shoes were the same shade of brown as the Gucci handbag which swung from its strap on her shoulder.

I stared at her as she came hurrying towards me.

'Hi, Charlie,' she said. 'You look great. Do you like my outfit?' And she twirled round on her toes to give me a better look.

'The handbag,' I said stonily. 'You said it was old-fashioned.'

'I changed my mind,' she said airily. 'It's not so bad when you get used to it.' And she wandered off to be admired by some new arrivals.

I could have kicked her. I was so mad I wanted to shove her in the flower bed and jump up and down on her. But I was even more mad with myself. Fancy being taken in by a trick like that. I must be getting soft in the head.

I saw my mum giving Angela and the Gucci

handbag a sharp look as we all got into line to set off for the church. But she only pursed her lips and shook her head slightly in my direction, and I expect she didn't want to start a scene in front of all the guests. Angela and I walked together, and you should have seen how she showed off as we walked along. Some boys even whistled at her outside the Corner Shop, and she giggled like anything and went all pink.

In the middle of the church service I suddenly decided I couldn't stand it any longer. She looked so good and innocent with her clasped hands and her bowed head that I felt like banging her on the head with my hymn book, and I knew it was no use trying to pray with such murderous thoughts in my mind.

So when everybody started clattering to their feet to sing 'The Lord Is My Shepherd' I slipped quietly away and ran home. I let myself in and dashed upstairs and flung myself down on my bed and had a good old howl.

I felt a lot better after that. I washed my blotchy red face and combed my hair and sat by the open window to let the breeze cool my cheeks. And it was while I was sitting there that I had the idea.

The more I thought about it the more I was sure it would work. In any case it was worth a try. I jumped up from the window and took a one pence piece from my purse.

I opened Angela's horrible red plastic handbag and looked inside. I had already noticed that there was a pocket with a mirror in it, and another smaller pocket sewn into the first one. I slipped the coin into the tiny secret pocket and went downstairs to the hall.

I knew they would all be getting back from the church by now, and luckily it was my dad who answered the phone.

'I was just coming to look for you, pet,' he said, sounding relieved. 'Are you all right?'

'I'm fine,' I said quickly. 'I was dying to go to the loo.' And I crossed my fingers behind my back because it was a fib.

My dad laughed. 'Too much excitement, I expect. Are you coming round for the celebrations? The food looks pretty good.'

'Yes, in a minute,' I said. 'But I'd like to tell

Angela something first, if she's there.'

'She's here,' said my dad. 'Hang on. I'll get her for you.'

I heard footsteps coming towards the phone and then Angela's voice.

'Charlie? Are you OK? Where did you disappear to?'

'Listen, Angela,' I said. 'I just want to check about the handbags. We did say no swoppies back, didn't we?'

'Definitely,' said Angela firmly. 'You can't change your mind now, Charlie Ellis.'

'Oh, good,' I said, making my voice sound all pleased. 'I was just making sure. And that includes everything inside the bag as well, doesn't it?'

'Of course it does,' said Angela. 'There's only a stupid old mirror.' There was a pause, and then she said, 'You haven't found anything else, have you, Charlie?'

'Only a secret little money pocket,' I said, and this time there was an even longer silence. I could almost hear her brain ticking.

'What money pocket?' she said. 'I didn't notice any money pocket.' And I started doing a little dance on the rug because she was falling for it.

'Well, it doesn't matter how much money I've found,' I said gleefully. 'We said no swoppies back.' Then I made myself sound all impressed. 'I didn't know your grandma in Blackpool was rich,' I said. 'Blimey, she must be rich as turkey gravy!'

I could hear her shouting as I banged down the phone. But I took no notice. I ran upstairs and sat on my bed to wait.

I didn't have to wait long. The back door suddenly squeaked open and Angela's voice floated up the stairs.

'Charlie? Charlie, are you there?'

'Up here,' I called. 'In my room.'

And there she was in my bedroom doorway, all out of breath from running. Her face was pink and sort of sheepish. And in her arms was my Gucci handbag.

'Sorry, Charlie,' she said. 'I know we said no swoppies back and everything. But my mum won't let me. She's doing her nut.'

She held out my bag towards me. 'It was a present, you see, that red handbag. It would upset my grandma if I gave it away. So if you don't mind . . .'

I didn't say anything. I just handed over the red bag and took mine back in exchange and I had an awful job keeping my face straight.

'What about the, er . . . money you found?' she said, dead casually as if she didn't really care. 'Is it still in the secret little pocket?'

'It's all there,' I said. 'Don't spend it all at once.'

I was dying to dance about and do cartwheels all over my bedroom. But I just put my lovely bag carefully away on a shelf in my wardrobe and we walked arm in arm down the drive and round to Angela's house.

We found the party in full swing, with everybody talking at once and swigging cups of tea and glasses of champagne and eating sausage rolls and anchovy toast and chicken sandwiches and telling Auntie Beth and Uncle Peter what a lovely baby they had. I went off to find my dad and to get myself something to eat, while Angela slipped quickly away upstairs.

It turned out to be one of the best parties I've ever been to, and we all had a great time. It was an awful shame that Angela's mum was called away in the middle of it to see to Angela, who had suddenly started to have some kind of a fit upstairs, screaming and shouting and swearing and stamping and throwing things at the wall. Nobody could understand whatever could be the matter with her.

Nobody except me, that is. And I certainly wasn't going to say anything. I had three salmon and cucumber sandwiches and two helpings of sherry trifle, and I didn't feel in the least ashamed of myself for playing such a dirty trick on my best friend. I reckon it served her right.

Some Other Puffins

MY BEST FIEND
Sheila Lavelle

Angela is Charlie's best friend, or best fiend as Charlie accidently wrote in her school essay. But fiend is probably a better word, as it's Angela's so-called marvellous ideas that always get Charlie into trouble. Like putting a spider in Miss McKenzie's sandwich, and plastering glue all over Laurence Parker's chair, and most fiendish of all, setting fire to her father's garage...

Friend or fiend, life is never dull for Charlie with Angela around in this, the first book of the hilarious and very popular fiend series.

CALAMITY WITH THE FIEND
Sheila Lavelle

With Angela around Charlie always finds herself in a whole heap of trouble. Whether it's a plan to kidnap a dog and then collect the reward, or claim first prize in a painting competition, Charlie finds herself up to her ears in one hilarious calamity after another.